Britta Teckentrup

Get Out of My Bath!

nosy crow

It's Ellie's bathtime.

Hello Ellie!

Ellie **loves** waves.
Can you help her make some?
Gently shake the book from
side to side and see what happens
when you turn the page . . .

Well done!

Look at those waves!
Ellie wants to play some more.
Now tilt the book to the left
and see what happens . . .

Hooray!

This is **fun!**
Now tilt the book to the right!

But what's this?

There's a **crocodile** in Ellie's bath! And he's taken Ellie's rubber duck. Ellie does **not** look happy. Can you shout,

"**Get out, Crocodile!**" Can you shout louder?

Oh dear!

That didn't work.
Crocodile is
still there!

And now Flamingo is in the bath, too!

And look . . .

Tiger has just
jumped in with a
great big . . .

Splash!

This bath is **very** crowded.
Surely no one else can fit in.

Eeek! **It's a mouse!** Now there really are too many animals in this bath. Let's try to shake them out. Start shaking!

Can you shake harder?

That hasn't helped at all! And it looks like
Ellie's had **enough**. She shouts,

"Get out of my bath!"

Can **you** shout too? But what is Ellie up to?
She's sucking up **all** the water with her
long trunk until . . .

. . . all of the
water has gone.

BBRRR!

The animals are shivering.
Can you shiver, too?
"Let's go!" they say,
and they all disappear.

And when Ellie is sure that the animals have **really** left . . .

she squirts all the water back into her bath!

Aaaahh!

Now there's **lots** of room
in Ellie's bath again.
Clever Ellie!

And thank you for helping.

Maybe it's time for
your bath now?

To Silke
– B.T.

First
published 2015
by Nosy Crow Ltd
The Crow's Nest,
14 Baden Place, Crosby
Row, London SE1 1YW
www.nosycrow.com
This edition published 2021
for Scottish Book Trust
ISBN 978 1 83994 537 3
Nosy Crow and associated logos are
trademarks and/or registered trademarks of
Nosy Crow Ltd.
Text and illustrations © Britta Teckentrup 2015
The right of Britta Teckentrup to be identified as
the author and illustrator of this work has
been asserted.

A CIP catalogue record for this book is available from the
British Library.

Papers used by Nosy Crow are made from
wood grown in sustainable forests.
Printed and bound in China

1 3 5 7 9 8 6 4 2